British Library Cataloguing in Publication Data
Arkle, Phyllis
The dinosaur field.
I. Title   II. Haines, Elizabeth   III. Series
823'.914 [J]

ISBN 0-340-49712-2

Text copyright © Phyllis Arkle 1989
Illustrations copyright © Hodder and Stoughton Ltd 1989

First published 1989

Published by Hodder and Stoughton Children's Books,
a division of Hodder and Stoughton Ltd,
Mill Road, Dunton Green, Sevenoaks, Kent TN13 2YA

Photoset by Litho Link Ltd, Welshpool, Powys, Wales

Printed in Great Britain by St Edmundsbury Press Ltd,
Bury St Edmunds, Suffolk

40p (42)

CHEETAHS

PHYLLIS ARKLE

The Dinosaur Field

illustrated by
Elizabeth Haines

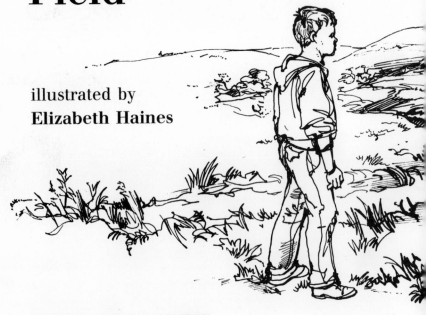

HODDER AND STOUGHTON
London Sydney Auckland Toronto

Contents

The Old Stone
Chapter 1

Rocky, the old old dinosaur, stirred and yawned. He raised his small head on the long neck and glanced round. Not a single fellow dinosaur in sight. But then, he hadn't seen one for millions and millions – hundreds of millions! – of years. He couldn't imagine where they had all gone, or why he, Rocky, was still here.

Perhaps it was because he had slept most of the time. Every five hundred years or so (when no one was looking) he walked just a few steps to stretch his limbs.

Nothing worried him. Food? Within his reach were berries, leaves, mushrooms and acorns. And he drank from the stream which ran almost alongside him. He was never without the comforting sound of running water.

Lonely? Never! Red deer came down from the surrounding hills, foxes and badgers scurried round him. Squirrels chattered as they ran along the branches above his head. Birds hovered. Cattle scratched themselves against his back.

All these creatures recognised Rocky,

but no one else knew that there was a *dinosaur* in Farmer Gregory's field.

Why should anyone know? With his head tucked into the side of his body and eyes closed he looked exactly like a gigantic stone, hard and smooth.

No one else knew there was a dinosaur in Farmer Gregory's field? Well, no one that is, except Ben, Farmer Gregory's grandson. And Rocky didn't mind Ben.

Voices! It was holiday time and Ben would be staying with his grandfather. Ben always came straight away to see Rocky.

'Rocky's still here!' shouted Ben, as he came running.

'Oh, that old stone,' laughed Grandpa.

'Not a stone, *not* a stone,' cried Ben, skipping about. 'I keep telling you, he's Rocky, the dinosaur. He must have been left behind when the rest of the dinosaurs disappeared.'

'That old stone has been here ever since I can remember,' said Grandpa. 'Probably carried down by the ice age. And it's never moved.'

'You've never *seen* him move!' cried Ben.

'All right, all right, have it your own way. It's Rocky, the sto ... I mean, the dinosaur,' said the farmer with a twinkle in his eye.

He turned away. Rocky opened one eye and stared at Ben. Ben smiled. When Ben

was little, very little, Rocky had opened
one eye, just a crack. From that time Ben
had had no doubt whatsoever that Rocky
was a dinosaur.

And he loved him.

'Come on, Ben!' called Grandpa.
'I've serious business to discuss with the
estate agent.' He pointed at a large cluster
of mushrooms. 'We'll gather those for
supper on our way back.'

Now, mushrooms were Rocky's favourite
food and he hadn't noticed that particular

clump. Slowly he swung his neck round so that, with a little effort, he managed to reach the mushrooms, which he ate until there wasn't a single stalk left. Then he went happily to sleep.

He awoke some time later when he heard raised voices.

'But you can't, you *can't* sell Rocky's field as building land,' Ben was shouting. 'He wouldn't be happy. He'd feel lost. He'd . . .'

'Now then, Ben, don't make a fuss,'

sighed Grandpa. 'I hate the idea of selling as much as you do, but times are hard and I'm desperately short of money.'

'But it's unfair to disturb Rocky after millions and millions of years,' cried Ben.

Grandpa shook his head and put an arm round the boy's shoulder. 'Do be reasonable, Ben,' he said. 'We'll pick the mush . . .' He looked down, puzzled. 'They've gone! Now who? . . . So far as I know there's been no one round here today.'

'Rocky's eaten them,' said Ben.

'Really!' shouted Grandpa. 'Well, perhaps you're going to tell me that stone ate my sprouts and the tops of my carrots last night, and the night before that. All I can say is we've no mushrooms and no sprouts, so you'll have to dig up some carrots if you want any supper!'

Out of the corner of one eye Rocky watched Ben and his grandfather climb over a stile on their way back to the farmhouse. Rocky was horrified. Buildings? He'd be lonely without his animal friends. There might be nothing left for him to eat –

and the thought of moving any distance terrified him.

All he wanted was to be left alone in peace.

Next morning Ben appeared with Grandpa and a stranger.

'My goodness, what a whopping stone!' heard Rocky.

'*Not* a sto–' began Ben.

'Yes, it's a landmark round here,' put in Grandpa hastily.

'Well, it takes up enough space for at least two houses,' said the stranger.

'But you couldn't possibly move it,' said Grandpa. 'I reckon it's been here for millions of years.'

'Millions and millions,' added Ben.

'We might try blowing it up with dynamite,' said the man.

'Oh, no, no, NO!' cried Ben, stamping his feet.

'Fond of that old stone, are you?' said the man, surprised.

Grandpa led the way on an inspection of the field. When they returned Rocky overheard the man ask, 'Any risk of flooding, underground streams or wells?'

'Oh no,' Grandpa assured him. 'Usually dry as a bone, this field.'

'Well, in my opinion it's an ideal site for houses,' said the man. 'I'll bring my surveyor along in the morning. Probably be able to make you a good cash-down offer straight away.'

The man left.

Ben stared at the ground as he and

Grandpa made their way back to the farm. Grandpa looked very thoughtful, but all he said was, 'My vegetables disappeared mysteriously again last night. We'll have none left if I don't catch the culprit soon.'

But Ben didn't care if he never ate another vegetable.

Rocky was very upset. Dynamite? Whatever next? He couldn't settle down for thinking about his problems.

Soon after midnight, as the moon came from behind a cloud, he heard an unusual noise. He raised his head and, to his surprise, saw two very tall creatures hopping about among the trees. They had rounded ears sticking straight up, and large hind legs. Never before had Rocky

set eyes on such weird-looking animals.

The old dinosaur was so curious that he started to rise on his haunches to take a closer look. But he was very, very stiff. As he tried to get to his feet he lost his balance, toppled over, and fell right across the stream. He lay helpless as the water surged round him and started to spread across the field, while the strange

16

creatures slipped silently away.

Hour after hour Rocky struggled to get up. He certainly didn't relish the prospect of being stuck in the stream for the next million years or so. At last, just before dawn, when he had almost given up hope, he managed to crawl out of the water and lower himself into his original position.

What a mess, he thought, as he glanced in dismay at the water which now covered a large part of the field. But he tucked in his head and, exhausted, fell asleep.

He was disturbed a few hours later. Rocky recognised the stranger's voice saying indignantly, 'But you told me this field was always dry. Look at it. Wet and soggy!'

'*I* can tell at a glance it's totally unsuitable for development,' said another man. 'I wouldn't even waste my time surveying it.'

'But this has *never* happened before,' cried poor Grandpa, bewildered.

Ben went over and rubbed his hand against the dinosaur's hard body. 'Rocky's awfully wet, Grandpa,' he said. 'He must have been – '

'What's that?' interrupted the strangers together.

'Oh nothing,' said Grandpa. 'Ben's always imagining things.'

The two men shrugged their shoulders and departed.

'Well, that's that,' said Grandpa. 'We'll never see those men again. I'd better find out what caused the flooding before another client appears.'

'But I was going to tell you. Rocky – ' began Ben.

'And I was going to tell *you*. Stop daydreaming about that old stone,' said Grandpa.

'But just look at the churned-up mud,' said Ben, pointing towards the stream.

'Cows,' said Grandpa. He sighed. 'Nothing but trouble at the moment. Ground waterlogged. No offer for the field. Crops stolen . . .'

'I'll help track down the thieves, really I will, Grandpa,' said Ben eagerly. 'I'll start right away.' He was feeling much happier.

But later on, when they were having supper, Grandpa spoiled everything.

'Someone interested in a factory site is coming to view the field later in the week,' he told his grandson.

Rocky has a Chill
Chapter 2

For the next few days Grandpa was busy about the farm, while Ben spent as much time as possible in the field with Rocky. But Ben was worried in more ways than one.

'I don't think Rocky's very well,' he told Grandpa. 'He doesn't even blink at me and I'm sure he's shivering. Do you think I ought to try and give him a dose of cough mixture or something?'

Grandpa raised his eyebrows. 'Oh, don't worry,' he said. 'That old stone will be here for many, many years to come.'

But Rocky *was* feeling ill. He must have caught a chill lying in the stream that night, he thought, as he tried to stifle a sneeze. Also, he had a pain in his stomach. He really shouldn't have eaten all the mushrooms. Greedy!

Someone coming. He lay quiet. Yet another stranger with Ben and Grandpa. Cause for alarm?

'My, what a massive stone!' heard Rocky.

'Everyone says that,' said Ben quickly. 'But he's *not* a – '

'Yes,' said Grandpa. 'I reckon that stone

weighs at least two thousand tons.'

After a thorough inspection of the field
the three paused again by Rocky.
He wished they would move away. He had
the greatest difficulty in holding back a
cough, or a sneeze – or both at the same
time – as well as expecting his stomach to
start rumbling any minute.

But the stranger would not be hurried.
He continued to gaze at the field,
the stream, the trees, the cattle. Then he
walked slowly all round Rocky.

'This stone really does take up a lot of
room,' he said.

'He belongs here more than any of us,'
said Ben.

'Er . . .yes, I suppose it does,' said the man as he continued to stare at Rocky. 'However,' he said at last, 'in spite of that obstacle, I consider the field an excellent site for our factory.'

Grandpa looked as though a great load had been lifted from his shoulders.
But Ben turned away. He couldn't bear to look at Rocky.

'It's getting late,' said Grandpa, glancing at his watch. 'We'll take our visitor home for supper, shall we, Ben?'

'But we haven't got any vegetables,' Ben reminded him.

'Oh, bread and cheese will suit me very well, thank you,' laughed the man.
'I've decided to stay at the Rose and Crown overnight, so I'll walk back across the field after supper.'

Off they went to the farm.

Rocky was very apprehensive. A factory? Sounded very unpleasant to him. Also he was still feeling ill.

Later on he became aware of rustlings in the bushes. Could it be those two oddities again? Yes! The big-eared creatures leapt out and hopped over to him. What strange animals they were, but how very friendly, thought Rocky, as they playfully pushed against him. Watching his new friends' antics the old dinosaur forgot his troubles for a while.

Until he heard whistling. The man on his way back to the inn, perhaps? The two creatures took refuge behind the dinosaur as the man climbed over the stile and walked towards them.

Rocky suddenly felt a strong tickling sensation in his nose and throat. He held his breath, but couldn't stop his stomach rumbling.

'Brr . . . brrrr . . . brrrrr . . . brrrrrr' it went, increasing in volume. The man, puzzled by this unusual sound, stopped in his tracks. There came a more menacing noise. A hissing, as Rocky failed to control a sneeze. It grew louder and louder before bursting out into a roar like a hurricane in full blast. Then came a cough like a shot from a gun.

At that moment two big bodies, looking almost white in the moonlight, appeared.

They gave a wondering glance at Rocky as they took a flying leap in the man's direction. He fell back, aghast. Then he turned, stumbled and fell, picked himself up and ran, screaming, to the village.

'Ghosts! Ghosts! Two of them. Tall, white, with glaring eyes,' he managed to gasp when he collapsed at the inn. 'And such an uncanny roaring – like devils on the loose.'

The landlord listened until he had finished. 'No ghosts round here,' he said, shaking his head in disbelief. 'Although we do get very high winds at times. You'll feel better after a good night's sleep.'

Protesting that he was telling the truth,
the man was led upstairs to his room. Next
morning he departed without even waiting
for breakfast, but not before he had spread
more tales of strange happenings in
Farmer Gregory's field.

Grandpa and Ben were having breakfast
next morning when the postman arrived.
The man was full of rumours of ghosts in
the farmer's field.

'Ghosts!' laughed Grandpa. 'In my field?'

'Yes,' nodded the postman. 'You had better go along to the village and find out what it's all about.'

So after breakfast Grandpa and Ben set off. Ben jumped over the stile in front of Grandpa, ran up to Rocky and patted his head, which was tucked in as usual.

'I'm sure Rocky's not better yet,' he told Grandpa.

'Sorry about that,' said Grandpa,

absently. 'But do come along, Ben.'

The Rose and Crown was unusually full of people that morning. They were listening intently to Mr Robson, the landlord, when Grandpa and Ben arrived.

'The man was absolutely petrified when he stumbled in here last night,' he was saying. 'So upset he could hardly get his words out properly.'

His wife joined in. 'He said two ghosts, at least four metres tall, with enormous ears and big staring eyes, appeared out of nowhere.'

'And the noise!' continued Mr Robson. 'First an uncanny rumbling coming from the depths of the earth. Then a slow hissing, which grew and grew into a sort of explosion.'

'And the earth trembled under his feet,' finished Mrs Robson.

Grandpa was not amused. He looked round at everybody. 'Any more exaggerated accounts of what supposedly happened in my field last night?' he asked. 'All *I* heard were a few claps of thunder in the distance.'

'I heard nothing,' put in Ben. 'But I expect Rock–'

'BEN!' cried Grandpa.

'I didn't believe what the man told me when he came in last night,' said Mr Robson, 'but he certainly convinced me this morning.'

'Well, it's all nonsense!' cried Grandpa. 'There are no ghosts in my field, nor anywhere else so far as I am aware.'

'I've often heard tales of there being a Roman settlement somewhere round here,' said a villager.

'Perhaps the man saw ghosts of two Romans,' suggested Mrs Robson.

'Really!' cried Grandpa. 'Romans? Four metres tall with enormous ears? More

likely two deer with long shadows. The man must have been drunk, although he was sober enough when he left the farm.'

'Oh, no, he wasn't drunk,' said the landlord.

Poor Grandpa. He grew more depressed as rumours of floods and hauntings in his field spread rapidly, and people declared *they* wouldn't risk crossing that field, even in broad daylight.

'I'm afraid no one is going to be interested in buying the field while these rumours persist,' the estate agent told Grandpa. 'You'll have to bide your time, Mr Gregory.'

Ben was sorry because Grandpa's financial problems seemed likely to

continue. But, on the other hand, he was
very glad that, so far, Rocky was safe.
It was all very difficult.

Grandpa was still puzzling over the
missing vegetables. 'To think that, for the

first time in my life, I am having to *buy* vegetables,' he said.

'I'm quite sure Rocky isn't the thief,' said Ben.

Grandpa ignored this remark. 'The whole vegetable plot is wired in against rabbits, so they can't be blamed,' he said.

'Perhaps the ghosts ate them,' said Ben.

'Nothing would surprise me,' said Grandpa, laughing a little.

Ben visited the field every day to talk to Rocky. It didn't bother him at all that he never got an answer. He knew Rocky understood every word he said. And he never once saw signs of ghosts or heard strange noises. But then, he never expected to.

Another week went by. Grandpa was beginning to think he would never sell the field. What then? How could he earn more money?

'Will you have to sell the farmhouse?' asked Ben, worried.

'Never,' said Grandpa. 'This house has been occupied by our family for nearly two hundred years.'

From Outer Space
Chapter 3

One day, however, two engineers called unexpectedly at the farm. They wanted to view the field, so Grandpa and Ben took them there straight away.

It did not take them long to give an opinion. 'This field will make an excellent site for engineering works,' one said.

'But that stone's rather in the way,' said the other. 'Don't know what we could do about it, though.'

'Paint it red, white and blue for a bit of fun. The workers would enjoy that,' said the first man.

Grandpa looked extremely disapproving and Ben, for once, was speechless with dismay.

'As there are several things to be considered before we make our final decision,' one man said, 'we've decided to stay in the village for a few days.'

'Explore the neighbourhood, check transport facilities, etcetera,' said the other. 'Where would you suggest we could stay?'

'Oh, the Rose and Crown in the village is very comfortable,' said Grandpa.

Ben felt especially unhappy. 'I just don't

trust them,' he told Grandpa when the
men had left.

'And why not?' said Grandpa.

Ben shook his head. He *knew*.

Next morning one of the villagers,
a shift-worker on his way home from night
duty, called at the farm. 'Mr Gregory,
I think you ought to know about
something going on in your field last
night,' he said.

'Oh, what was that?' asked Grandpa.

'Well, I was taking the short cut when
I noticed two men acting suspiciously,'
he went on.

Ben glanced at Grandpa.

'They were walking very, very slowly
across the field and shone a torch on the
ground all the time. I kept well out of
sight on the other side of the hedge.'

'Hmm . . .' said Grandpa, stroking his
chin and looking very thoughtful.

'I was right not to trust those engineers,'
cried Ben.

'Don't jump to conclusions,' said
Grandpa. 'They were probably testing the
ground for some reason.'

'What! So late at night?' said the shift-
worker.

'Well, er ... if it continues, I'll have to inform the police, but for the time being I'll wait and see what happens. All the same, thank you for telling me.'

But Ben was very suspicious.

And so was Rocky.

For last night he had noticed the men walking slowly, zig-zag fashion, towards him from the far end of the field. What on earth were they doing at this time of night, he had wondered. After about two hours they had covered less then half the field. Would they continue until they reached him? But the men stopped, put out the torch and returned to the village.

Rocky had heaved a sigh of relief before relaxing.

But next night, when the moon was full, the men appeared again. Starting where they had left off the previous night they walked slowly towards Rocky, examining the ground inch by inch by the light of the torch.

As they drew nearer Rocky noticed that one man carried a spade, but he couldn't make out what the other was holding.

They stopped by Rocky.

'I don't think it's any use going all round this old stone,' said one man. 'The ground's too rough. The instrument won't work. Let's give up.'

'No, we'll have to go on trying,' said the other stubbornly.

When they had walked full circle round Rocky, one man threw down his spade in disgust. 'I told you all along we were on a wild-goose chase,' he grumbled. 'There's nothing here.'

'I don't agree,' said the other. 'This field was pin-pointed on the old map I told you about. Somehow we must have missed finding it. We'll have to go all over the field again.'

(Whatever could 'it' be? wondered Rocky.)

'Not on your life!' shouted the first man. 'I've had enough. This place gives me the creeps.'

'Ssh,' warned his companion.

'And don't "Ssh" me,' said the other. 'I'm off.'

He turned to go and stumbled over Rocky's big toe, which was sticking out. At that moment two tall creatures, with long shadows stretching out behind them, burst out of the bushes.

The men jumped. One, startled by the apparitions, hurled the instrument he was carrying towards the animals. It hit one on the shoulder before dropping into the undergrowth. Both animals, in a panic, rushed back into the bushes.

Rocky, infuriated by this harsh treatment of his friends, didn't even stop to think what he was doing. With neck reared,

head held high and eyes blazing he moved just a few paces towards the terrified men, before sinking to the ground again.

It was enough. The men started back in horror and bumped into one another as they rushed off towards the village.

Rocky settled down in his new position. He was tired. Apart from the night when he had fallen into the stream, it was the first time for over five hundred years that he had actually moved!

Next morning Grandpa and Ben heard the news that the men had left the village. Grandpa sighed. 'It sounds to me as though another transaction has fallen through.'

'Never mind, Grandpa,' said Ben. 'We'll find a solution somehow.'

Grandpa finished the milking before he and Ben set off for the village. To their surprise they came across a group of people in the field near Rocky. The village constable was there, as well as Mr and Mrs Robson from the Rose and Crown.

Mr Robson told them what had happened. 'I thought everyone had gone to

bed when I locked up last night, but later
on I heard hammering on the front door.
Those two engineers looked absolutely
horror-struck when I let them in.'

'They started packing immediately,' said
Mrs Robson, 'and advised us to alert the
whole village and flee the place.'

'And what was the cause of all this
commotion?' Grandpa wanted to know.

'When I could get any sense out of them
it appeared that they had seen an
horrendous sight in your field,' said
Mr Robson.

'*Here?* Not again!' cried Grandpa.

The man nodded. 'Right here,' he said.
'A spaceship landed alongside them.'
He pointed at Rocky. 'Just in front of that
giant stone. It had two brilliant lights on

top of something rather like a periscope.'

'That would be Rocky's –' said Ben.

'That would be an aircraft overhead getting ready for landing,' said Grandpa.

'But that's not all,' continued the man. 'They said two weird-looking aliens from outer space leapt out of the ship and made straight for them.'

'Nonsense!' cried Grandpa.

'Oh no, Mr Gregory, they actually described the aliens. Enormous ears, big hind legs and standing at least four metres high,' said Mr Robson.

'And pouches,' added his wife.

'*Pouches!*' roared Grandpa. 'Sound to me like a couple of kangaroos. Plenty of those round here. Ha-ha!'

'Must have burrowed their way up from

Australia,' put in Ben, enjoying the joke.

'Well, it's a mystery,' said the constable. 'Perhaps we'll never know the answer. But there's no doubt those men were up to no good traipsing about your field in the middle of the night.'

He bent down and picked up a spade lying on the ground. 'This belong to you, Mr Gregory?'

Grandpa examined the spade. 'Not mine,' he said.

'It must have been left behind by one of those men,' said the constable.

'Perhaps he was using it to dig a tunnel for the kangaroos to go back down under, to Australia,' said Ben.

Even Grandpa laughed at that.

The constable gazed at Rocky. 'I bet that old stone could tell us what really happened,' he said.

'*He* certainly could,' agreed Ben. 'You see, he's not a–'

'It's a boulder brought down during the ice age,' said Grandpa quickly. 'But all these tales of ghosts will not help the sale of my field.'

'Don't worry,' said the constable. 'I'll start enquiries. Try to get to the bottom of the matter.'

'Oh, but this field has always been a spooky place,' said Mrs Robson.

'Nonsense!' cried Grandpa yet again. 'There must be a rational explanation.'

Rocky is Annoyed
Chapter 4

For the next few days Grandpa and Ben tried to forget their worries by working very hard. One day towards the end of the week the constable joined them in the field. He looked round and shook his head. 'I really can't imagine ghosts in this peaceful environment,' he said.

'Nor can I,' said Grandpa.

'I've been making enquiries over a wide area,' the man went on, 'and no one has reported seeing anything unusual.
I'm baffled.'

'I'd like to see a kangaroo,' said Ben.

'As much chance of seeing a yeti as a kangaroo,' laughed Grandpa.

'Farmer Jones has a cow with three horns – that's unusual,' said Ben.

'Well, she's unlikely to be roaming round in the middle of the night, is she now?' said the constable, with a grin.

'Oh, by the way,' said Grandpa, changing the subject. 'I've got some eggs ready for you. Ben, run and fetch a dozen, there's a good lad. They're on the kitchen table.'

Ben set off at a good pace. 'Don't *run* on the way back,' Grandpa called after him.

Ben soon returned, carrying the carton of eggs against his chest. He wasn't very pleased to see the constable sitting right on top of Rocky's head. Still, the man wasn't very heavy.

'Thank you, Ben,' said the constable as he took the eggs. 'As I was saying, Mr Gregory, I don't think this old rock is responsible for the lack of interest in your field. Agreed, it takes up a lot of space, but that can't be helped.'

'He –' began Ben.

'Ben thinks it's dinosaur-shaped,' said Grandpa.

The constable laughed as he swivelled round to look up at Rocky. 'Hmm ... perhaps,' he said. 'What great, useless, ugly creatures dinosaurs must have been.'

Now, although Rocky's brain was no larger than a hen's egg and he rarely bothered about what humans said, he didn't like the sound of this conversation. Ugly? Useless? A sudden swift jerk of the dinosaur's head – seen only by Ben – and the constable lay sprawled on the ground.

Ben stood wide-eyed. Beyond doubt this was the most exciting event of his whole life. So far he had only noticed Rocky's eyelids open and close. But now he'd actually seen his head move. What a day to remember!

Grandpa rushed to help the man to his feet. 'Whatever happened?' he asked anxiously.

'I must have slipped off the rock,' said the constable ruefully. 'And look at the eggs – all smashed!'

'Oh, soon replace those,' said Grandpa. 'Ben, run back and bring another carton.'

It didn't take Ben long to get to the farm, and return with the eggs.
The constable soon left, promising to continue with his enquiries.

'Can't think how he managed to slip off that protruding rock,' said Grandpa, scratching his head.

'He didn't slip,' Ben told him. 'Rocky pushed him.' And he ran off before Grandpa had a chance to say anything.

Ben climbed up the hillside and sat down at the top. Below him in the field he

could see Grandpa and Rocky and, beyond,
the farm buildings. Of all the holidays he
had spent with Grandpa this was the most
wonderful. He wished it could go on for
ever and ever. He refused even to think
about the field being sold.

Suddenly he noticed a figure climbing
over the stile, and recognised Mr Robson
from the Rose and Crown. Wonder what
he wants, thought Ben, as he started back
down the hill.

'All this talk of hauntings is affecting my
trade, as well as leaving you short of offers
for the land,' Mr Robson was saying as
Ben joined them. 'People are too scared
even to cross the field to the inn.'

'I'm sorry,' said Grandpa, 'but I don't know what I can do about it. All these rumours are nonsense, of course.'

'That may be so, but people round here are very superstitious,' said Mr Robson. He looked up at Rocky. 'Perhaps this great monstrosity has something to do with it.' He gave Rocky a whack with a stick he was carrying.

'This old stone is a great asset to the neighbourhood,' said Grandpa. 'When I was young my grandfather told me he believed it was brought down in the ice age, and Ben has always shown great interest in it.'

'Well, in my opinion, it's hideous and a blot on the landscape,' said the landlord.

He turned to go and Grandpa moved
after him, arguing in Rocky's defence.
They didn't get very far. Rocky's brain was
working full time. And he was very, very
angry. Hideous? Blot on the landscape?

Ben watched fascinated as the great
beast suddenly reared his small head on
the long neck and, leaning forward,
prodded the landlord hard in the back.

Taken by surprise, the man stumbled,
fell down the slope and landed right in the
middle of the stream. Grandpa and Ben
ran and helped him out. Soaked to the

skin, Mr Robson stood shivering as the water poured off him.

He looked puzzled. 'I must have caught my foot on a stone, but . . .' he put a hand to his back '. . . something seemed to hit me right here.'

He looked accusingly at Ben.

'Oh, it wasn't me, Mr Robson,' said Ben hastily.

'Ben wouldn't dream of doing such a thing,' said Grandpa.

'Well, I don't know what my wife's going to say,' said Mr Robson glumly. 'She'll never believe I just *fell* into the water.'

'Perhaps she'll think you've been drink –' began Ben brightly.

'What you need is a shower and some dry clothes,' interrupted Grandpa. 'Come home with us and we'll put you to rights.'

Back at the farm Mr Robson undressed and went under the shower. First Ben rung out the wet garments, then put them in the drier. Grandpa prepared coffee. Soon all three were sitting down at the kitchen table, drinking coffee and eating biscuits.

'It's very, very strange – mysterious,' said
Mr Robson. 'I can't imagine what
happened to me in the field.'

Ben opened his mouth but shut it
quickly when he caught Grandpa looking
at him.

'I shouldn't worry,' said Grandpa.
'No one need know what happened.'

Grandpa and Ben walked back to the
village with the landlord. They left him,
still looking perplexed, at the door of the
Rose and Crown.

Grandpa was rather despondent.
'We seem to be getting nowhere fast,'
he said. 'No buyers – and no solution to
the "ghost" problem.'

But one morning when Ben was making

an early-morning cup of tea for Grandpa, who was in the yard, he heard an announcement over the local radio:

'Wandering wallabies again. Will anyone catching sight of two wallabies please contact Mr Wayman of Westgate on 20972, or the police.'

Ben quickly wrote the name and telephone number on a piece of scrap paper before running into the yard to tell Grandpa about the message.

'Bless my soul – wallabies?' exclaimed Grandpa. 'Not ghosts! Mr Wayman of where, did you say?'

'Westgate,' said Ben, very excited.

'That's quite a journey for two hopping wallabies,' said Grandpa. 'I'll phone the constable. We'll keep watch in the field tonight in case the animals come back here.'

As soon as it was dark Grandpa and Ben, joined by the constable, hid near the stile. It was not very long before they heard rustling and were soon rewarded by the sight of two wallabies hopping out of the bushes.

'They're not *very* tall,' whispered Ben.

'They look very tall when they stand upright on their hind legs,' said Grandpa.

At that moment the two wallabies did just that.

'Two tall "ghosts",' chuckled the constable.

Ben hugged himself in delight as he watched the animals playing round Rocky. 'They're Rocky's friends,' he whispered.

Grandpa led the way back to the farm.
The constable phoned Westgate 20972 and
in under an hour Mr Wayman arrived,
driving a horse-box. Ben went along to the
field with the others and watched as the
wallabies were easily caught and coaxed
into the box.

'They're very friendly creatures,'
Mr Wayman told them, 'and never object
to being caught.'

'Did you buy them in Australia?'
Ben wanted to know.

'Oh no,' said Mr Wayman. 'They were
born in a zoo, which unfortunately had to
close. No one wanted them, so I built a
high-wire fence round my garden. That's
home to the wallabies now.'

'Except when they're here,' said Ben.

'They'll be visiting you again, for certain,'
smiled Mr Wayman. 'High as it is, they

leap over the fence when they want to.'
He turned to Grandpa. 'By the way,
Mr Gregory,' he said. 'I understand my
wallabies have been eating your vegetables.
Next time I come I'll bring a good supply
of vegetables, which you can keep in your
deep-freeze.'

Grandpa laughed. 'That's very kind of
you,' he said.

Ben was sorry to see Mr Wayman leave.
But in two days time he was back again –
to collect his wandering wallabies.

And he had not forgotten his promise
about the vegetables.

Treasure
Chapter 5

It was nearly the end of Ben's holiday.
No one had been to look at the field.
One day he was playing near Rocky while
Grandpa worked in the field. He threw a
ball up high. It sailed right over the
dinosaur's back and disappeared from
view.

Ben ran round and on his hands and
knees started searching in the long grass.
No luck. So he crawled under some prickly
bushes and suddenly had to duck to avoid
something hanging above his head.

Looking up through the tangled
branches he saw a long-handled thing
stuck in the greenery. With some difficulty
he managed to pull it down and drag it
out into the open. On examination it
looked rather like a vacuum cleaner.

He called to Grandpa, 'Come and see
what I've found.'

Grandpa studied it carefully. 'I think it's
a type of metal detector,' he said at last.

They looked at one another as the same
thought struck them. Ben was first to
speak. 'It was probably what those
engineers were using,' he said.

'You may be right,' said Grandpa.

'But what were they looking for?' said Ben.

'Ah, that's what we'd like to know,' said Grandpa. 'Anyhow, I'll report to the police when we get home.'

He showed Ben how to operate the detector before he went back to work. Ben tested it by moving it slowly over the ground. He had an idea.

'Grandpa,' he called again. 'I'm going to start at the far end and cover the whole field to see if I can find anything interesting.'

'If there had been anything those men would have detected it,' said Grandpa.

'No harm in trying,' said Ben.

'That's the spirit,' said Grandpa.

Carrying the detector, Ben quickly made his way to the far end of the field. Then he turned and started walking very slowly towards Rocky, moving the instrument from side to side as he went. It was hard work and slow going. After an hour he had covered less than a quarter of the field and was quite relieved when Grandpa

called, 'Lunch! Time to stop, Ben.'

After a quick meal at the farm Ben, determined to finish the job, started off again. He stopped to rest occasionally and it was late afternoon when he reached Rocky.

Grandpa had finished work. 'I should give up now, Ben,' he advised. 'The

ground round the stone is too rough and
overgrown. I don't think you'd get a
positive response from the detector even if
there was something there.'

But Ben was determined. 'I'll just try,'
he said.

Grandpa waited as Ben started to walk
round Rocky, holding the detector as near
to the ground as possible. When he was
halfway round he stopped and gasped.

'Grandpa! Grandpa!' he shouted.

Grandpa came running.

'Look!' said Ben pointing at a smooth
piece of ground alongside Rocky. 'Rocky's
moved. And I didn't notice until now.'

'Moved?' said Grandpa. 'Impossible.'

'But he *has*,' insisted Ben. 'Just here.'
He bent down and pointed again. 'At least
half a metre.'

Grandpa looked up at Rocky, then down

at Ben kneeling on the space until recently occupied by the dinosaur's left thigh. 'Well, er . . . it might – only *might* – have moved a little due to the flooding,' he said.

Watched by Grandpa, Ben picked up the detector again and began moving it over the empty space. Suddenly he shouted, 'It's sort of trembling and making a funny noise,' he shouted. 'What does that mean, Grandpa?'

Grandpa took hold of the instrument and moved it as Ben had done. With the same response.

'I guess there is metal buried in the ground here,' he said. 'But I warn you not to get excited, it might be only ten pence pieces or parts of some old farm machinery.'

'But we'll have to dig and find out what it is, won't we?' said Ben, full of excitement. 'I'll go and get a spade.'

'Wait, Ben,' said Grandpa. 'Let me think for a minute.'

Ben waited impatiently.

'Those two engineers were after something valuable they thought was hidden in my field,' said Grandpa. 'Agreed, Ben?'

'Yes,' nodded Ben.

'They didn't find it . . .' said Grandpa.

'. . . because Rocky hadn't moved then,' said Ben quickly.

'But that doesn't mean there isn't anything to find,' Grandpa went on. 'I've decided to ask Mr Scott's advice before we start digging on our own. He knows all about Roman settlements and antiquities.'

Mr Scott, the archaeologist, was very interested when he heard the news. 'I'll be along in the morning,' he promised.

Next morning Grandpa and Ben were out early. They hadn't long to wait for Mr Scott, who soon got to work with the metal detector.

'There *is* something here,' he cried, after he had tested the ground. 'If you agree, Mr Gregory, I'll bring my experts to organise a dig.'

'You won't disturb Rock–?' began Ben.

'That stone won't be in the way?' asked
Grandpa.

'Oh no,' Mr Scott assured them.
'I've often thought it would be a good idea
to get a Preservation Order on the stone.
One rarely finds rocks of that age and size
in this part of the country.'

'Would that mean he would be quite
safe?' Ben wanted to know.

'Of course,' said Mr Scott.

That weekend a four-man team started
digging. Ben was allowed to watch. He was
determined to see that Rocky came to no
harm.

The team made very careful
preparations before starting to dig, then
shored up the sides of the hole with wood
as they went deeper and deeper into the
ground. It seemed a very long time to Ben

before a muffled cry from the bottom of
the hole was heard.

'I've found something!'

They waited breathlessly as, one by one,
dirt-encrusted gold, silver and bronze
pieces were brought to the surface. Very
carefully, Mr Scott scraped mud off some
of the items. 'Necklaces, pendants and
bracelets, as well as rings, and a horde of
Roman coins,' he announced. '*And* pottery.
A superb find, Mr Gregory!'

'Will they all belong to Grandpa?' asked
Ben.

Grandpa laughed.

'I'm afraid not, Ben,' said Mr Scott.
'The treasure will belong to the Crown.
However, I'm sure your grandfather will
be entitled to a handsome reward for
discovering treasure of such historical
importance.'

'Will Grandpa be able to keep the field?'
asked Ben anxiously.

'Certainly,' said Mr Scott. 'As a site of a
Roman settlement this field is very
valuable.'

'Does that mean it will never be built
on?' said Ben.

'Never,' replied Mr Scott.

It was the end of the holiday. Everything
had turned out happily for Grandpa and
Ben – and Rocky.

Ben wanted Grandpa to let him tell
everyone about the dinosaur's part in
finding the treasure.

But, 'No,' said Grandpa. 'If it is a . . .'

'*He,*' Ben reminded him.

Grandpa started again. 'If he is a
dinosaur, it will be wise to let him go on
sleeping. Just think what would happen if
you told everyone about him. Curious
people would overrun the field. Stare at
him. Most likely, though, he would have to
go to a zoo – a very large zoo! – or
perhaps be shipped to America, or
somewhere further away. It . . . *he* wouldn't
like that.'

'No, he wouldn't,' said Ben, after some thought. 'Rocky loves it here with all the animals and birds, and me every holiday.'

'And two vegetable-eating wandering wallabies,' laughed Grandpa.

'I expect it will be at least another five hundred years before Rocky moves again,' said Ben.

'Oh, another million years before he wakes up again,' said Grandpa, giving the dinosaur a good long look.

The way I feel now it will be at least *two* million years before I move again, thought Rocky, who had been awake all the time.

And so, no one knew there was a dinosaur in Farmer Gregory's field.

No one, that is, except Ben.

And – perhaps, Grandpa?